Run Like Hell

God Bless You!!

Chris Holloway, Sr.

ISBN-10: 1717263119

ISBN-13: 978-1717263117

2 CHRONICLES 7:14

If my people, who are called by my name, will humble themselves and pray and seek my face and turn from their wicked ways, then I will hear from heaven, and I will forgive their sin and will heal their land.

Table of Contents

2 CHRONICLES 7:14 3

Table of Contents 4

Exposition 5

The Dream: In its Entirety 8

Chapter 1: The Smoke. The Fire. The Debris.   13
    The Dream, Part One:
        The Smoke   16
        The Fire   20
        The Debris   24

Chapter 2 :The Lurking Lioness   28
    The Dream Part Two:

Chapter 3 : The Opposite Direction   36
    The Dream Part Three:

Chapter 4 : The Lion Possum   43
    The Dream Part Four:

Chapter 5 : The Only Safe Place   51
    The Dream Part Five:

About the Author   63

Exposition

Therefore, come out from among unbelievers, and separate yourselves from them, says the Lord . Don't touch their filthy things, and I will welcome you.

2 Corinthians 6:17 NLT

The first law we see in the book of Genesis after God says, "let there be light", is the law of separation. Why does God establish a law of separation in the beginning? The answer is simple, distinction. God emphasizes the difference between light and darkness so that there is no confusion called the middle.

That's because there is no middle with God. It is either right or wrong. Good or bad. Pleasing or unpleasant. There is no gray with God because he despises lukewarmness. In the book of Revelation, God said, "I would rather you be hot or cold." Distinction is necessary because the mind cannot conceive that which cannot be identified.

When one understands the difference between two things no one can pollute his or her mind into believing something is other than what God has created it to be. A dog's bark doesn't sound like a cat's meow. God distinguishes to prevent deception caused by perversion.

Perversions have contaminated the minds of the people, creating a unisex gospel that is misconstrued as being alright in the eyes of God. This is why today many have a difficult time distinguishing right from wrong, light from darkness, good from evil, and men from women. A church without distinction is heavily polluted with sin because sin is the mingling of good and evil.

God separates the two Satan mingles them. It's time for the church to run like hell.

-LeVaughn Flanders, Jr.,

The Dream: In its Entirety

On April 18, 2018 at 2:37, I woke up from one of the most horrific dreams I've had in a long time. I don't recall how it started or what sparked it; all I know is that there was a fire. It was a fire so massive that it not only threatened to consume me – well, *us* – in the dream; but when I awakened from the dream, the smell of smoke and fire lingered in my room.

From what I could tell, we were in an area along the interstate with deep woods on either side. The fire started out small but grew with such intensity that we were forced to vacate our vehicles and run. There were many of us running, but those whose faces I remember vividly were my loved ones, some family and some church members. Among them were: Serena, ShaKerra, Trevon, Ashley, Bubbles, Jacob and Shannon. The others were merely silhouettes in a sea of smoke. The fire quickly began to surround us, with ash and debris flying in multiple directions. We ended up running into LaQuanda, another church member, who was next to what seemed to be an abandoned car repeating, "I need this car. The man said I can get it on Tuesday."

I grabbed her by the arm and said, "Come on. There's a fire, but we will stop and get the car."

As we resumed our attempt to dodge the smoldering fire, I noticed what seemed to be a lioness lurking off to the side in a wooded area. She was nearly invisible through the smoggy smoke; but when I realized that the faint figure was a 200 pound beast, I turned my flashlight onto her until she was distracted and ran away.

As we continued to run, we came across, Shawntea, a former church member, who was running in the opposite direction. I grabbed her by the arm and cried, "Baby! Daughter! Come with us," but she kept shaking her head with an affirmative, "no".

"I know you are concerned about The Badgett's," I pleaded, "but trust me, they were right behind us." I finally convinced her to come with us, and when I glanced back, I noticed the flames moving closer and closer. Its heat consuming and killing many in its path.

We eventually came to a residential area off of a hill, and as we trekked it, I began to grow weary. I held my wife Serena's hand and said, "Baby, pray for me because I'm getting really tired and I don't know if I can make it!"

Immediately she started praying and decreeing, "God, give him strength to get through this!"

Finally, we made it up the hill, but when we got to the houses, LaQuanda said, "That's the house with my car." We stopped, and there was a chain-linked fence around the front yard and a large box that had been a bit wet from the water sprayed by the rescue helicopters on the front porch. I jumped the fence and went to move the box when a large male lion jumped out at me! Before it could attack me though, the smoke choked it, and it fell over. Whether it died or just passed out, I don't know.

As the chase between the fire and us continued, and we were running down the hill, we noticed an opening that I came to realize was the "safe place" with a lake in the distance. Somehow Serena, Tea, and I got separated from the others. A gut-wrenching feeling of hurt and pain ran through me, but we kept on running.

A few minutes later, I saw Jacob running towards the safe zone, and I yelled out his name. He turned, looked directly at me, ran towards me, and leaped into my arms. As we looked behind us, we saw Shannon carrying Bubbles (or Baby Serena), who was so weary that she bordered on being delusional. Still, I kept saying to my wife, "baby, we made it!"

Finally safe, I began a head count – reciting the names of those faces I saw vividly. I can't remember if ShaKerra and Trevon made it because at that point I was undone, wailing hysterically in my sleep and repeating, "Lord help us! So many people are dying! Help us!"

I felt myself growing more alert as my body jerked and twitched. It was Serena shaking me to consciousness. "Baby wake up! Wake up! You are dreaming!" When I finally came to, I was surrounded in a pool of my own sweat and tears. Then a voice said unto me, "It's time to run like hell."

Chapter 1: The Smoke. The Fire. The Debris.

The Dream, Part One:

"The fire started out small but grew with such intensity that we were forced to vacate our vehicles and run."

As I petitioned God to reveal the meaning of this dream, immediately the Spirit spoke the words, "the beginning." As I sat down to write this book, I knew that many would not understand this revelation; however, those who love to define words and put their deeper meaning into perspective, can relate. The phrase "the beginning" can also be defined as "the start of." When it comes to life-changing moments, like the devasting fire in this dream, it is easy to fall into the trap of assessing the damage – or focusing on the aftermath. But God showed me that the focal point of this dream does not hinge on what happened after the fire was set ablaze but rather what caused it. If a person, or a church, or a spiritual leader focuses on preventing a massive fire or disastrous situation, then the risk of a devastating aftermath is a non issue. And just as the "fire started out small but grew with intensity", Satan is counting on us to ignore the smallest details because even he knows that it's the small foxes that destroy the vine. In our case, this small fox, or this beginning, is with our mouths!

"Behold, we put bits in the horses' mouths, that they may obey us; and we turn about their whole body. 4 Behold also the ships, which though they be so great, and are driven of fierce winds, yet are they turned about with a very small helm, whithersoever the governor listeth. 5 Even so the tongue is a little member, and boasteth great things. Behold, how great a

---

matter a little fire kindleth! 6 And the tongue is a fire, a world of iniquity: so is the tongue among our members, that it defileth the whole body, and setteth on fire the course of nature; and it is set on fire of hell. 7 For every kind of beasts, and of birds, and of serpents, and of things in the sea, is tamed, and hath been tamed of mankind: 8 But the tongue can no man tame; it is an unruly evil, full of deadly poison."

James 3:3-8 KJV

The voice of God is speaking boldly in this hour, commanding me to warn those whose mouths are on fire! We are living amongst a people who are speaking great things with swelling words, but God has said, "Those are the words of the flesh and not of my Spirit!"

The Smoke

The serpent in the Garden of Eden was more subtle and sagacious than any other beast that God had created – it was a master deceiver and manipulator. What people may not realize though is that the serpent, who would come to be known as Satan himself, did not speak one lie during his conversation with Eve. While it was true that if they ate of the fruit, they wouldn't die, he failed to mention that God was talking about a spiritual death and separation – not a physical one. He spoke the truth undergirded with deception.

This is because deception will never present itself as a lie nor will it tell the whole story. Instead, its purpose is to get one to believe something by twisting facts and through manipulation. In this case, the hope of deception is to get one twisted and tangled up again with the yolk of sin. Cloaking itself attractively, it feeds its victim just enough to grab his or her attention. It knows that no one wants something that he or she doesn't find attractive!

"Now the serpent was more subtil than any beast of the field which the Lord God had made. And he said unto the woman, Yea, hath God said, Ye shall not eat of every tree of the garden? 2 And the woman said unto the serpent, We may eat of the fruit of the trees of the garden: 3 But of the fruit of the tree which is in the midst of the garden, God hath said, Ye shall not eat of it, neither shall ye touch it, lest ye die. 4 And the serpent said unto the woman, Ye shall not surely die: 5 For God doth know that in the day ye eat thereof, then your eyes

shall be opened, and ye shall be as gods, knowing good and evil."

Eve's greatest mistake then, was conversing with that snake at all. Just like many of us, whether in the past or in the present, Eve was beguiled and seduced into foolish chatter; and it took only one question for Satan's power of domination to be effective: *"Did God say that you shall not eat of every tree in the garden?"* This tactic is what I call, "Questions of Justification." These are the questions in which believers of Christ should be wary. These are the questions that lead to the slippery slope of justifying sin. But my God told me to warn the people, "Repent because great judgement is about to come upon this land!" Because people have made sin justifiable and are working to make His Word obsolete, God said, "My people have been blinded by the smoke of deception!"

"But be not deceived; God is not mocked: for whatsoever a man soweth, that shall he also reap" (Galatians 6:7).

I beseech you therefore children of the most high God, don't get hell's smoke confused with heaven's cloud! Follow the cloud of God: it will lead you, cover you, and protect you during the hour of desolation that is on its way!

The Fire

Now the Spirit speaketh expressly, that in the latter times some shall depart from the faith, giving heed to seducing spirits, and doctrines of devils; 2 Speaking lies in hypocrisy; having their conscience seared with a hot iron."

1 Timothy 4:1-2

Deception begins in the heart but is produced by the tongue, and there are so many people who have great influence but with a deceptive tongue. I often teach that God will never speak to you through the voice of man, a new revelation, but he will speak a word of confirmation. This is what makes some prophets of God, or even those who proclaim, "God told me to tell you", problematic.

"By these words, saith the Lord, my people have given ear to seducing spirits and have departed from what they know is right."

1 Timothy 4:1

Not everyone who speaks in the name of God is of God nor is sent by God, but this is not something to be brushed off. With their false interpretation of God's word, their tongues kindle an uncontainable fire. The flattering lips of these false prophets suck believers into a web of deception – we are now in that dispensation of the great falling away.

.   If the only thing one's leader, shepherd, pastor, teacher, or preacher has to offer are words of prosperity and never a word of correction, then he or she must reevaluate his or her leadership. And though prosperity is the believer's portion as the Apostle John said in his writings, *"Beloved, I wish above all* things that thou mayest prosper and be in good health, even as thy soul prospereth" (3 John 1:2 KJV), as leaders we still have been commanded to reproach our flock as it is written in the book of Ezekiel: "When I say unto the wicked, Thou shalt surely die; and thou givest him not warning, nor speakest to warn the wicked from his wicked way, to save his life; the same wicked man shall die in his iniquity; but his blood will I require at thine hand" (Ezekiel 3:18).

This begs the question, how can people be so gullible and believe something that Biblically makes no sense? Well, the Spirit of God spoke this to me, "People fall for what makes no biblical sense because what they're seeking is Hope!" Satan loves to catch people in this vulnerable state to manipulate them; and his tongue is the false hope that ultimately leaves people devastated.

"Let no man deceive you with vain words: for because of these things cometh the wrath of God upon the children of disobedience."

Ephesians 5:6

The Debris

Much like the inquiry above, another comes to mind: *do these false prophets care about the wellbeing of those whom they leave devastated?* This reminds me of the debris in my dream that remained after the fire. The word debris is defined as being "the remains of something broken down or destroyed; something discarded." People who entertain, and worse, act upon, false hope are like this debris – but worse. They are wounded, broken, and destroyed by putting their faith in the scorching words of manipulation.

I, too, have been a victim of this. There was a time when I needed a word from the Lord to help guide me through some tough decisions, and I received what I thought had been spiritual advice from someone I trusted. I later learned that I was being manipulated for their own selfish reasons; this "guidance" ended up being destructive for both my physical and spiritual well-being. This happened on more than one occasion.

Now, some may be saying, "he should've learned from his first mistake," and they would be right; but it's easier said than done. This just further proves the devious subtlety of manipulation. It keeps its victims ignorant and only has his or her destruction in mind.

Satan knows that the more one trusts him, the more devastated he or she becomes; and his ultimate goal is accomplished if he persuades The Church to betray their leaders's trust, resulting in his or her words to be diluted. Keep in mind, though, not all preachers can be deceived. There are some who have either experienced or witnessed this deception enough to know when it rears its ugly head. It is up to you then, reader, to learn the difference.

"And we beseech you, brethren, to know them which labour among you, and are over you in the Lord, and admonish you."

1 Thessalonians 5:12 KJV

We are living amongst a gullible generation, lacking knowledge and understanding of the authentic voice of God. In other words, like the Scripture says, "hell is being enlarged" because God's voice is imitated so well. The consequences of this are never immediate because of the burgeoning lack of spiritual discernment. One ultimately doesn't recognize his or her demise until well after the damage has been done.

"But every man is tempted, when he is drawn away of his own lust, and enticed. 15 Then when lust hath conceived, it

bringeth forth sin: and sin, when it is finished, bringeth forth death."

James 1:14-15

Don't become the casualty of someone else's war. Don't become the debris that's left behind after others have depleted you. Grab hold to the Word of God. The Prophecy: "Many will be consumed and left desolate because of their lack of knowledge concerning my Word," saith God. "This generation shall see many spiritual casualties. Many shall die in their spirit for living according to the flesh. Repent while it is yet day!"

Chapter 2 The Lurking Lioness

The Dream Part Two:

As we resumed our attempt to dodge the smoldering fire, I noticed what seemed to be a lioness lurking off to the side in a wooded area. She was nearly invisible through the smoggy smoke; but when I realized that the faint figure was a 200 pound beast, I turned my flashlight onto her until she was distracted and ran away.

"For among my people are found wicked men: they lay wait, as he that setteth snares; they set a trap, they catch men. 27 As a cage is full of birds, so are their houses full of deceit: therefore they are become great, and waxen rich."

Jeremiah 5:26-27 KJV

Even though this chapter (and part of the dream) are the shortest of this book, it may very well be the most controversial. This section of the dream picks up where we are desperately trying to flee from this intense fire. At this point, the fire had become overwhelming, and we were moments away from being consumed – but not by the fire; by *the smoke*.

Fire melts and chars the body's exterior, but it's the smoke that smothers and consumes the body's interior. This is why many may escape a fire with few burns, believing that they are in the clear, but ultimately die because of smoke inhalation, sometimes without the doctor's even noticing. This is also what sometimes makes smoke more dangerous than the fire itself. It has the potential of being lethal without leaving any visible signs!

The aforementioned chapter asserts that deception is first manufactured in the heart but is manifested through the tongue. Some may understandably be wondering, *what does this have to do with the lioness?* Well, it has been revealed to me that God is about to expose those who have been hiding and lurking behind the smoke; in other words, those who have been operating in the spirit of deception. Others may ask, "would a loving God such as ours really expose his people?" The answer to that is, yes. One cannot hide the accursed thing from the Creator, expecting he won't know! Let's consider the Biblical Achan.

"And he brought his household man by man; and Achan, the son of Carmi, the son of Zabdi, the son of Zerah, of the tribe of Judah, was taken. 19 And Joshua said unto Achan, my son, give, I pray thee, glory to the Lord God of Israel, and make confession unto him; and tell me now what thou hast done; hide it not from me. 20 And Achan answered Joshua, and said,

---

Indeed I have sinned against the Lord God of

Israel, and thus and thus have I done:"

Joshua 7:18-20 KJV

This brings me to the lioness in the dream. When I asked God what the lioness symbolized, His Spirit responded that, "the lioness, the female lion, is somewhat likened to the gender of a person, but moreso, it's a bold representation of the characteristics of the spirit of deception." In Eden, Satan chose to direct his temptation towards Eve, the woman, first. Before I continue, I do not intend for what follows to be misconstrued as a woman-bashing crusade. Rather it is to illustrate that Satan targeted the more vulnerable vessel knowing that she was also the most dedicated. Satan had a plan from the very beginning.

During counseling sessions, I often tell married couples that a woman knows a man better than he really knows himself. This is because God created man from the dust of the earth, but the woman was created from the *rib* of the man. It was during this time that she was adorned with both male and female instincts, with dual senses and abilities. This is why Queen Esther was able to stand in the courts and gain the attention of the King (**Esther 5:1-2**) and why Sampson so willingly gave up his secret after lying in Delilah's lap (**Judges 16:15-17**).

"Now the serpent was more subtil than any beast of the field which the Lord God had made. And he said unto the woman, Yea, hath God said, Ye shall not eat of every tree of the garden?"

Genesis 3:1

The word subtle is defined as being cunning, crafty or sagacious. Again, this is why Satan approached Eve first and not Adam. It's because women have a stronger ability to be deceptive than men. Satan knew the superior seductive prowess of Eve before she knew it herself. It was that cunning potential that satan was after!

"For such people are false apostles, deceitful workers, masquerading as apostles of Christ. 14 And no marvel; for Satan himself is transformed into an angel of light. 15 Therefore, it is no great thing if his ministers also be transformed as the ministers of righteousness; whose end shall be according to their works."

2 Corinthian 11:13- 15

The purpose of deception is to merge the gifts that one is impregnated with, with fear and doubt so that these gifts, whether in the form of a vision, a ministry, or something else, is stillborn. Deception will allow one to give birth to his or her gift, but that gift will be dead on arrival.

Even though women had to take more of a background role in the early church and society, they are now more powerful than ever. This begs the question, *could the Antichrist come in the form of a woman?* Consider what's taking place in the world of entertainment. There have been remakes of several movies from the late 80's and 90's, such as *Ghostbusters* and *Oceans 11*, that had all male leads. In the remakes of these movies, however, the roles have been reversed from having strong male leads, to having strong female leads.

The latest version of the *Oceans 11* series, *Oceans 8*, has the same plot as its predecessor; but instead of an all male cast playing the leading roles, a cast made up of all women play them. It is also no coincidence that this version backtracks and starts with *Oceans 8*. The world of entertainment is a breeding ground for anti-religious sentiments. This can be witnessed through songs, videos, movies, etc. The subliminal Satan instigates is that time is repeating itself.

Mankind's eyes were open to their sin nature after Eve's disobedience, and now time has rewound itself back to that same point. One can debate this point to exhaustion, but disobedience began with Eve and continued with Adam. It was because of this disobedience that mankind can continue to live but with consequences and punishment. In short, when one observes what is occuring in the entertainment industry, the role reversal between men and women signifies that society is closer to the second coming of Christ and judgement. The more sin and abominations that become acceptable according to this world's standards, the swifter God's judgement will be.

Chapter 3: The Opposite Direction

The Dream Part Three:

As we continued to run, we came across Shawntea, my daughter in spirit, who was running in the opposite direction. I grabbed her by the arm and cried, "Baby! Daughter! Come with us," but she kept shaking her head with an affirmative, "no".

"I know you are concerned about The Badgett's," I pleaded, "but trust me, they were right behind us." I finally convinced her to come with us, and when I glanced back, I noticed the flames moving closer and closer. Its heat consuming and killing many in its path.

"But if our gospel be hid, it is hid to them that are lost: 4 In whom the God of this world hath blinded the minds of them

which believe not, lest the light of the glorious gospel of

Christ, who is the image of God, should shine unto them."

2 Corinthians 4:3-4

In my prayers about this part of the dream, God showed me that it would also serve as encouragement to those who feel as though their efforts to gain souls for the Kingdom of God is in vain. This is because we are living in a time where most leaders are more concerned with filling up pews and seats than filling up souls with salvation. Whenever I think of this, I find myself diligently praying, "Lord, use me to lead your people *to a Christ* rather than to a church." If only we as leaders and believers in Christ Jesus would become more concerned about the spirit of a man and not his gifts, talents and resources, then we would all be more successful at winning souls!

Therefore my people are gone into captivity, because they have no knowledge: and their honourable men are famished, and their multitude dried up with thirst. 14 Therefore hell hath enlarged herself, and opened her mouth without measure: and their glory, and their multitude, and their pomp, and he that rejoiceth, shall descend into it. 15 And the mean man shall be brought down, and the mighty man shall be humbled, and the eyes of the lofty shall be humbled: 16 But the LORD of hosts shall be exalted in judgment, and God that is holy shall be sanctified in righteousness.

Isaiah 5:13- 16

Previously I asserted that "hell has been enlarged". Have you ever wondered why? Society has been warned time and time again since the Prophets of old, until this very hour, that we are living in our last days. Sin has become more accessible, acceptable, and justifiable, leaving the standard of holy and righteous living diluted and rendered ineffective. Society's carnal culture has adopted the nonsense theology that one can somehow live however he or she chooses and still be in good graces with God. If this were the case, then there would have been no need for Jesus to hang on the cross; there would be no need for repentance.

No one is exempt. We have all sinned at some point in our lives. However, there is a difference between willful sin and being overtaken by it. Because man is simply spirit clothed in flesh, the risk of falling into temptation, into sin, is more probable. Fortunately, with God's grace and the keeping power of his Holy Spirit, we can fight against the power of temptation and live a Godly lifestyle.

This is why the turning back, the running towards the fire, poses the risk of one losing his or her soul in the process. There are many biblical testaments that serve as an example of why it's hazardous for God's people to return to their old ways. Remember Lot's wife? In Genesis, God laid out specific consequences for her because of her desire to look back at a city that God was in the process of destroying. God spoke to me and said, *"Tell this people that judgement is nigh. Even at the door. For I have given them space to repent and turn from the very thing that they're turning towards."*

Further, In the Gospel writings of Luke 9:62, Jesus himself said, "No man, having put his hand to the plough, and looking back, is fit for the kingdom of God." Then in this same Gospel, Jesus gives us another stern reminder, decreeing, "No servant can serve two masters: for either he will hate the one and love the other; or else he will hold to the one and despise the other. You cannot serve God and mammon."

It was then that God's warning became frighteningly urgent. His words a cacophonous echo as he spoke more expressively: "My delay is an opportunity to repent and pray! Many shall fall into the snare of the wicked one, because thou hast taken my time for granted." Because of the delay concerning the promise of his Second Coming, many have lost their focus and have forgotten their purpose. The fire that once burned bright and deep is no longer illuminated. Many more will be consumed by the flames of sin, leading to their self-inflicted demise.

"What shall we say then? Shall we continue in sin, that grace may abound? 2 God forbid. How shall we, that are dead to sin, live any longer therein? 3 Know ye not, that so many of us that were baptized into Jesus Christ was baptized into his death? 4 Therefore we are buried with him by baptism into death: that like as Christ was raised up from

the dead by the glory of the Father, even so we also should

walk in newness of life."

Romans 6:1- 4

At some point, one must ask him or herself, *What is consuming me? What has me running in the opposite direction of God's voice?* It was Jesus who said in John 10:27, "My sheep hear my voice, and I know them, and they follow me." Destruction shall come upon those who are disobedient and judgement upon those who fail to follow the voice of God.

There is no need to fear, though. Those who are secretly sinning and leading God's people to the path of deception and falsehood are being exposed. They are coming to the forefront and being called by name, and the Lord will realign the purpose of those who desire to please Him by following his commands.

Chapter 4 The Lion Possum

The Dream Part Four:

Finally, we made it up the hill, but when we got to the houses, LaQuanda said, "That's the house with my car." We stopped, and there was a chain-linked fence around the front yard and a large box that had been a bit wet from the water sprayed by the rescue helicopters on the front porch. I jumped the fence and went to move the box when a large male lion jumped out at me! Before it could attack me though, the smoke choked it, and it fell over. Whether it died or just passed out, I don't know.

As the chase between the fire and us continued, and we were running down the hill, we noticed an opening that I came to realize was the "safe place" with a lake in the distance. Somehow Serena, Tea, and I got separated from the others. A gut-

wrenching feeling of hurt and pain ran through me, but we kept

on running.

"This second epistle, beloved, I now write unto you; in both

which I stir up your pure minds by way of remembrance: 2

That ye may be mindful of the words which were spoken

before by the holy prophets, and of the commandment of us

the apostles of the LORD and Saviour: 3 Knowing this first,

that there shall come in the last days scoffers, walking after

their own lusts, 4 And saying, Where is the promise of his

coming? for since the fathers fell asleep, all things continue

as they were from the beginning of the creation."

2 Peter 3:1-4

In this part of the dream, the Holy Spirit confronts me with

deception as it relates to my place within the church. Since the

beginning of time, Satan, who is described in scripture as being "the prince of the air and of this world", has been very strategic in his game plan. Think about it, how many times have you read in the Bible about a demon fighting a demon? It has always been kingdoms against kingdoms, religion against religion.

Though we made it to the top of the hill in the dream, it was the lion underneath the box on one of the porches that provoked the greatest revelation. The majestic and formidable lion, King of the jungle, is anyone in leadership or anyone who operates in any area of authority. Although some lions embody the nobility of a true ruler, there are others who are overly concerned with their titles, using their throne for nothing more than pomp and prestige. There is a spirit of rebellion, disguised as a spirit of help, that has come and settled into the church, deceiving many and causing them to turn from the truth of God's word. But, I have heard the voice of God instructing me to warn the wicked leaders that judgement is nigh.

Woe be unto the pastors that destroy and scatter the sheep of my pasture! saith the LORD 2 Therefore thus saith the Lord God of Israel against the pastors that feed my people; Ye have scattered my flock, and driven them away, and have not visited them: behold, I will visit upon you the evil of your doings, saith the Lord. 3 And I will gather the remnant of my flock out of all countries whither I have driven them and will bring them again to their folds; and they shall be fruitful and increase. 4 And I will set up shepherds over them which shall feed them: and they shall fear no more, nor be dismayed, neither shall they be lacking, saith the LORD.

Jeremiah 23:1-4

In the previous chapter, I detailed my running up a hill and how after awhile I begin to feel as if I couldn't make it any further. It was then that I asked my wife to pray for me, which she did. Not long after that, we made it to the top. On the other side of this, God showed me that there is a shortage of people who genuinely care about their fellow Christian brothers and sisters. Instead of basing their doctrine upon Scripture, prayer, and supplication, they have what is called a "leech anointing". Their motive is to reach their objectives by draining others dry – physically, emotionally, and ultimately, *spiritually*.

Fortunately, says the Lord, we are now in a season of Great Exposure. The lion in the box being soaked by the water from above and lunging at me powerlessly represents those who have authority but are on the verge of being uncovered. This uncovering, says God, is going to be of those who have polluted and tainted His word by way of their secret sins. But I hear the Lord saying unto his people, "Be not surprised at the revealing of those who stand and preach in my name but has fallen into the temptation of the tempter."

God has been preparing a remnant of people for a time such as this. He is calling them to the forefront to lift the box and expose the lion. "But set your face like flint," says God. "Because while you're taking a stand for my truth, it won't be the world that comes for you; it will be the preachers, the prophets, and those who hold titles *in name only.* But as they set out to pounce on you, to destroy you, I will cause them to faint under my anointing that is within you," says God!

Another revelation that I received concerning this lion was the significance of his being on the porch. A porch serves as a gathering place upon entry or exit of a building or edifice. The regal lion, who archetypically paces his kingdom with serene assiduousness, is more than a watchman: he is a guardian. God spoke to me, "My leaders are supposed to be on guard, to watch over and to protect what comes in and what exits my house. But because of the current condition of the Five Fold, satanic spirits have gained access to what is supposed to be inaccessible."

Because there is no power at the gate, unclean spirits have come in and occupied the space that was meant for the

Spirit of God. Considering the current state of the church, can one distinguish between it and the world? The leaders of the church, especially the pastors, have become more fearful of man than of God because they seek popularity over power. But God has commanded me to speak unto the Keepers of the Gate, "Every spirit that you have allowed to enter into his temple, first have to pass by you."

Back when my weekends consisted of trips to the nightclub, there were some that were considered "exclusive". In order to get into these clubs, either your name had to be on the list or you had to know someone with the authority to say, "Let em' Through!" This is the same for the church when it comes down to spiritual demons. They can only gain access to the House of God through someone who they know or with someone whom they are familiar.

In Job 2:1 it tells the story of how the Sons of God went to present themselves before the Lord and how Satan came with them so he too could present himself before the Lord. This explains how demonic spirits gain access to God's Kingdom. They enter by way of those who have familiar spirits. Because popularity takes precedence over power, the watchman is no longer serving as guarding, pacing the Kingdom with fortitude and protection.

God spoke to me and said, "Those who carry titles are not ignorant to the demonic spirits that are plaguing my church." Those who are supposed to uphold God's standards, according to his Holy Word, are allowing all manner of ungodliness and spirits of perversion to occupy His Holy Space. Because they are allowing such things, God will visit their iniquities with judgement that only repentance can reverse.

Chapter 5 : The Only Safe Place

The Dream Part Five:

Finally safe, I began a head count – reciting the names of those faces I saw vividly. I can't remember if ShaKerra and Trevon made it because at that point I was wailing hysterically in my sleep while repeating, "Lord help us! So many people dying! Help us!"

"Not everyone that saith unto me, Lord, Lord, shall enter into the kingdom of heaven; but he that doeth the will of my Father which is in heaven. 22 Many will say to me in that day, Lord, Lord, have we not prophesied in thy name? and in thy name have cast out devils?

and in thy name done many wonderful works?

23 And then will I profess unto them, I never

knew you: depart from me, ye that work

iniquity.

Matthew 7:21-23

Not everyone is going to Heaven. I know that seems a

harsh thing to say. But Biblically, its true. It was in this part of the

dream, the final part, that the Spirit of God nudged me

concerning the "End Times." A lot of people don't believe the

Scriptures that speak about the Last Days, but hopefully this

chapter pricks the minds of those who are incredulous. Also, as

you read this chapter, I encourage you to ponder this question:

"What if you die and get to the Judgement Throne of God only to

find out that your interpretation of sin was wrong and that old crazy preacher was right when he said, 'Repent, for the Kingdom of Heaven is at hand.'"

It is important to note that God will never interfere with a person's freewill. Whatever a person does or says, God intends for it to be his or her own choice. This is especially true as it relates to choosing God. Time and again in the Bible, God has made it clear that we are to love Him with all of our hearts, all of our soul, and with all of our might (Deuteronomy 6:5). He desires our love and affection, but he also wants it to be *our* choice in whether or not he receives it. He wants *us* to choose whether or not we live for Him or whether or not we commune with Him. One even has the liberty of believing what is written in His Holy Scriptures or dismissing it altogether. Keep in mind though, on the other side of choice is consequence. With every decision there is an outcome. This may be a tough pill to swallow, but much of a person's circumstances are a reflection of the decisions that he or she has made.

In the dream, when I looked up and saw Jacob running towards the safe zone, and I began to call his name, he turned, ran towards me, and leaped into my arms. God revealed to me that the significance of this is twofold. The first part is the safe place and what it signifies. As I began to meditate on this, the text Proverbs 18:10 came to mind, *"**The name of the Lord is a strong tower: the righteous runneth into it and is safe"** (Proverbs 18:10).*

When reading this text, one could argue that the strong tower is only a place for the righteous. But in truth, the name of The Lord is the *only* safe place. According to Acts 4:12, *"Neither is there salvation in any other: for there is no other name under heaven given unto men whereby we must be saved."* Those who are righteous recognize that there is safety, as well as power, in that name.

When Jacob heard me calling his name, he ran and leaped into my arms. That was because my voice projected safety. It brought a sense of relief to his troubled mind. But, it was not only my voice that did this for him, something else was at work.

Jacob also responded because he heard his *name*. He knew his name, and so did I. And I didn't simply know of him – I knew *him*. I shouted his name with such strength and urgency, that he couldn't help but turn around. This sentiment is also true when we think of God's role in our lives. *Does God know you, or does he simply know of you?* Does He call you by name?

So, what is that line that delineates between a person knowing someone rather than just knowing *of* them? Not all will agree, but it is in the relationship two people have with one another. Having a genuine relationship produces a mutual understanding and intimacy that builds trust. But when a relationship is non existent, when two people don't really know each other, all that's left to know is a person's name. And since it is one's name that is associated with his or her character, it is important to ponder the thought: *What am I known by?* In this last hour or in these last days, what legacy will your name leave?

"A good name is rather to be chosen than great riches, and loving favour rather than silver and gold."

Proverbs 22:1

In reading this Proverb, it is evident that having a good name is also a *choice*. It is only the person holding the name who can choose whether or not it has credibility. In order to do that, though, he or she must identify and eliminate the things that are infecting it. Doing this becomes one of the greatest challenges of an individual's life since the very thing (or person) one has attached to his or her name, even if that thing assassinates the person character, is the hardest to let go. In essence, we become immune to our toxicity.

"Be not deceived: evil communications corrupt good manners. "

1 Corinthians 15:33 KJV

Though in other texts or scriptures the word "communication" has a singular definition, the pluralized, "communications" here in 1 Corinthians 15:33 signifies a dual meaning. The contextual meaning here is conversation *and* lifestyle. We have all heard the saying, "birds of a feather, flock together." Oftentimes, we find ourselves in situations that have consequences beyond our control, but because of our association with certain individuals, the stigmas associated with their names become ours too. I had to learn this the hard way. I had people who I thought were a safe haven turn out to be shaky ground. I found myself crossing rivers for people who wouldn't even cross dry land for me. It was during a crucial time such is this when I found the Lord. It was then that I found out that Jesus is the only safe place!

Whether a person chooses to believe it or not, we are quickly approaching the end of this era. Jesus is on his way back! Only this time he is not coming as a redeemer but as a resurrector. He's not coming back as a reconciler but as rewarder of things good and things bad. For in that day the great trumpet shall sound and Jesus will crack the sky. The dead in Christ shall rise first, then they that remain shall be caught up to meet him in the middle of the air, and forever shall we be with the Lord.

Therefore, one must analyze his or her current relationship with God and also evaluate his or her earthly associations. It will be a sad day at the judgement because many will not make in heaven where God dwells. When there is no authentic relationship with God, or when one only knows *of* God, he or she is no longer in the arc of safety with Him. Whether a person accepts it or not, God is only obligated to those who are in a covenant relationship with Him, anyone else only has a grace connection; which is when people honor God with their lips, but their hearts are far from him. Because God has a genuine love for His children, His creation, and because it is his desire that all men should be saved, He gives them grace; He gives them time to repent and turn from that which is evil.

The snare of Satan that will trap many is one's own interpretation of what sin is even though it is clearly defined in the word of God. Yes, all have sinned and come short of God's glory, but the Apostle Paul poses an important question in Romans Chapter 6 when he says, "What shall we say then? Shall we continue in sin, that Grace may abound?" He went on to say, "God forbid. How shall we that are dead to sin, live any longer therein?"

Even though David made it clear in Psalm 51:5: "Behold I was shapen in iniquity and in sin did my mother conceive me," sin was never intended to become a dwelling place for those who believe in God. Sin is never to be committed simply because Jesus has become the propitiation for it.

While the earth remains and life is still anew, sin will forever be a challenge because no one is perfect nor will they ever be – that is until we meet our savior Jesus Christ. Concerning this portion of the dream, God told me to declare unto his people, "No matter how hard things may be, you must continue to run for safety. No matter how hot things may become around you, you must continue to run for cover!" While I continued to talk with the Holy Spirit of God, He showed me something simple yet has caused major eruptions in the lives of His people. I saw many running in the wrong direction, but the few that made it only did so because they trusted in the directions of the leader.

"This is the stone which was set at nought of you builders, which is become the head of the corner. 12 Neither is there salvation in any other: for there is none other name under heaven given among men, whereby we must be saved."

Acts 4:11-12

In our case, the name of the leader is Jesus. Even though many have said, "There is more than one way to God and Jesus can't be the only way," as it is written in the Word, one cannot bypass Jesus to get to God.

So, I encourage you, do not miss heaven based upon the opinions of man. Do not miss heaven because of self-righteous interpretations of God's word.Trust in what God has said and believe His word as it is written. Make holiness a priority in your life. Call on the Name of the Lord out of a pure heart. Repent, and, "Run Like Hell."

About the Author

Bishop Chris Holloway, Sr. has a tremendous passion for God's word coupled with a love for God's people. He has a contagious spirit of generosity that flows through every facet of his ministry. The field of evangelism is his passion and first love, where his heart and greatest concern is to draw people to "a Christ and not necessarily to a church". Bishop Holloway answered the call to preach on January 21, 1996 and accepted his first Pastoral assignment in October 2007.

Having received his mandate from God, Bishop Holloway launched Divine Worship Christian Center on November 4, 2011, which is where he currently, and obediently, fulfills his calling as Senior Pastor. On October 23, 2016 Holloway was consecrated to the Holy Office of Bishop. Humbled by this tremendous responsibility, it is his desire to hear God say, "Well Done!"

Study Notes

Study Notes

Study Notes

Study Notes

Study Notes

Study Notes

Study Notes

Study Notes

Study Notes

Study Notes

Made in the USA
Monee, IL
24 February 2020